For Susan, Nitsa, and Walaa —A.S.

For Felix, Jens, and Elfe.
Thank you for opening my eyes to so many different things. —P.-Y.C.

The parable of the three rings lies at the heart of Gotthold Ephraim Lessing's play
Nathan der Weise. With this he shows a way to achieve tolerance among the three
major world religions Judaism, Christianity, and Islam. Out of this landmark of
world literature Antonie Schneider weaves her own ring parable for children.

Antonie Schneider was born in Mindelheim (Allgäu), Germany, and even as a child she had a passion for books and stories.
She has now published more than sixty books, which have been translated into many languages and, together with her
poems both for children and for adults, have earned her international recognition. Her many awards include the Prix
Chronos, the National Parenting Award, and the Austrian State Prize. Today she lives as a freelance writer in what is known
as the Dreiländereck—where Germany, Austria, and Switzerland share their borders.

Pei-Yu Chang was born in Taipeh, Taiwan, where she studied German language, culture, and literature. On her completion
of a masters degree, she traveled to Germany to begin work on a doctorate on Chaos Theory in Literary Studies at
Münster University. There she discovered her passion for book illustration. In 2012, she took courses in the Department of
Communications Design and Illustration at the Fachhochschule in Münster. She is the author of *Mr. Benjamin's Suitcase
of Secrets*. She lives and works in Münster, Germany.

Text copyright © 2019 by Antonie Schneider.
Illustrations copyright © 2019 by Pei-Yu Chang.
First published in Switzerland under the title *Wem gehört der Schnee?*
English text copyright © 2019 by NorthSouth Books, Inc., New York 10016.
Translated by David Henry Wilson.

First published in the United States, Great Britain, Canada, Australia, and New Zealand in 2019 by NorthSouth Books, Inc.,
an imprint of NordSüd Verlag AG, CH-8050 Zürich, Switzerland.

Distributed in the United States by NorthSouth Books, Inc., New York 10016.
Library of Congress Cataloging-in-Publication Data is available.
ISBN: 978-0-7358-4320-2 (trade edition)

1 3 5 7 9 · 10 8 6 4 2
Printed in Latvia by Livonia Print, Riga, 2019.
www.northsouth.com

FSC
www.fsc.org
MIX
Paper from
responsible sources
FSC® C002795

3 9957 00211 7931

ANTONIE SCHNEIDER
PEI-YU CHANG

SNOW
FOR
EVERYONE!

Translated by David Henry Wilson

North
South

When it snows in Jerusalem, the camels are surprised.

The tops of the church towers turn white. The Dome of
the Rock wears a white cap, and the Wailing Wall is covered
with a white blanket.

The children celebrate because there's no school when
it snows. And it rarely snows in Jerusalem.

But last night in Jerusalem, it snowed.

Now it is morning, and the soldiers, traders, worshippers, pilgrims, and tourists all hurry through the snow-covered alleyways.

The soldiers carry their weapons, the nuns gather up their robes, the faithful hold on to their hats, and the tourists take photographs.

The church bells ring, the muezzin calls the faithful to prayer, and the traders offer their goods for sale.

The children play in the narrow lanes and divide up the precious snow.

"You can go there," Samir says to Rafi.

"This is the border," says Mira, using a stick to draw a line in the snow.

Rafi, Mira, and Samir pile up their snow and stand guard over it.

But the snow begins to melt.

The children look at the snow in their hands. They can't see any difference, but surely there must be a difference.

The snow is white. Simply white.

"We must find out which is the real snow," says Mira.

"And who it belongs to," adds Rafi.

"I'll ask the imam," says Samir. "He'll know the answer!"
He runs to the mosque with the snow in his hands.
"I'll ask the priest," says Mira. "He'll know the answer."
She runs to the church carrying the snow in her cap.
"I'll ask the rabbi," says Rafi. He fills his rucksack with
snow and runs to the synagogue.

"Show me the snow,"
says the priest.
   But all Mira has in her
hands is a wet cap.

"Show me the snow,"
says the imam.
   But all Samir has in
his hands is water.

"Show me the snow,"
says the rabbi.
    But all Rafi has in his hands
is a dripping rucksack.

"The snow is a mystery," says the rabbi.
"A mystery like God himself," says the imam. "He is there, but you cannot hold him."
"If you try to grasp the mystery," says the priest, "you lose it."

The children are sad. The
return empty-handed to the alleywa
Now there is nothing but a trickl
of water flowing over the cobblestone
"Where has the snow gone?" asks Mir
"We should have enjoyed it while i
was here," says Rafi.

We should just have
played with it," says Samir.
Now it's gone," says Mira.
And no one knows when it will come back again," says
Rafi. Everyone knows that it rarely snows in Jerusalem.
It's now evening. The children go home,
          thinking deep thoughts.

Suddenly, it starts to snow again!
Everyone hurries outside and wonders at it. The rabbi,
the imam, the priest, the soldiers, the faithful, the pilgrims,
the tourists, the traders, the animals, and even the roses look up
and wonder at it.

All is still.
And there is enough
snow for everyone.